It was almost nighttime in the Neighborhood of Make-Believe, but Daniel Tiger wasn't going to bed. Something special was happening: Daniel was going to a special storytime at the library . . . at night! He had been waiting all day, and now it was finally time to go to the library.

"Look how beautiful the sky is," said Mom Tiger.

"It is grr-ific," said Daniel. "But . . . why is it so many different colors?"

"Well, the sky changes colors when the sun goes down. Day is turning into night," said Dad Tiger.

"Good-bye, sun," said Daniel.
"Good-bye, sun," said Mom.
"Good-bye, sun," said Dad.

Daniel looked up into the night sky. "Look at all the stars," he whispered.

"I think we should walk to the library," said Mom Tiger, "so we can take our time and see all the things that are special at night."

"Tigertastic. Let's find out what's special at night," said Daniel.

"It's a beautiful night in the neighborhood," sang Daniel and his family as they began their walk to the library.

As Daniel walked through the neighborhood he heard many different sounds.

In the grass Daniel heard: *ribbet, ribbet, ribbet.*

It was a frog!

Up in a tree Daniel heard: *tweet, tweet, tweet.*

It was a nightingale!

On the ground Daniel heard:
chirp, chirp, chirp.

It was crickets.

"There are so many different noises at night,"
said Daniel.

The Tiger Family walked down Main Street.

"Everything is so dark," said Daniel. "All the lights are out at Music Man Stan's Music Shop."

"Most of the shops are closed at night," said Mom.

"Look!" Daniel gasped. "I see a light in the bakery! Let's go look inside!"

Daniel peered in the window of the bakery and saw Baker Aker rolling out some dough.

"What is Baker Aker doing?" Daniel asked.

"He's making bread so it will be fresh for the neighbors tomorrow," said Dad.

"Oh," said Daniel. "I didn't know he did that. Goodnight, Baker Aker."

The Tiger Family kept walking toward the library in the calm, cool night.

"Look, Daniel," said Mom. "The fireflies come out to play at night!"

Daniel looked, and he saw a group of fireflies flying around.

"Margaret and I will play with you, fireflies!" Daniel giggled.

"Daniel, look at all the stars," said Dad.

Daniel looked up at the sky. "There are so many stars, but I only see them at night. Where do they go during the day?"

"They are always there," said Dad, "but we can only see them when it's dark."

"I like looking at the stars," said Daniel.

"Me too," said Dad. "I like to look for pictures in the stars. Like . . . those stars look like a bear. But you have to use your imagination to see it."

When Daniel used his imagination, he could see the pictures in the stars. Daniel made believe that he was playing with the stars in the sky.

At last the Tiger Family arrived at the library.
"We're here!" exclaimed Daniel. "It's time for the pajama party!"

When Daniel walked into the library, he saw his friends.

"Hi, toots!" said Miss Elaina. "I'm wearing my pajamas in the library!"

"Me too!" giggled Daniel.

"Me three!" said Prince Wednesday.

"Hoo hoo. Tonight we're going to do everything in our pajamas," said O the Owl.

And that is exactly what they did.

First they sang a song and danced in their pajamas.

Then they played a game in their pajamas.

Finally they listened to a story in their pajamas.

When the story was over, it was time for everyone to go home and go to bed.

"But . . . I'm not sleepy!" said Miss Elaina. But then she gave a big yawn. "Okay, maybe I'm a little sleepy."

"Don't fall asleep yet," said Music Man Stan. "You don't want to miss a nighttime ride on Trolley."

Ding! Ding! Trolley rolled through the Neighborhood of Make-Believe, taking each of the neighbors home to their beds.

Thanks for coming to the library with me tonight. I like being out at night. Did you? Goodnight, neighbor. Ugga Mugga.